BUTTERFLY BOY

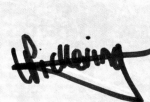

Written by
Toria Pickering

Illustrated by
Lera Munoz

For William and Tobias,
my inspiration and constant sunshine
T.P.

Oliver tiptoed quietly into his mummy's room and
lay down gently next to her.
She had been sleeping a lot. Oliver knew it was
because his mummy was poorly.

She had been unwell all
summer and he longed for her
to be better. He hoped that
she would be able to lift him
again and fly him through the
air, just like she used to.

As he gazed at the bright sunshine bursting through the window, something caught Oliver's eye. He hopped out of bed to closely inspect it.

"Mummy, Mummy, look!" he whispered to her.
She lifted her tired head from the pillow.
"A tiny caterpillar!" said Oliver. "He looks very weak.
He needs help! Can I keep him?"

His mummy nodded. "But you
must take good care of him."
"I promise," Oliver said excitedly.
"My first ever pet! I'm going to
help him grow to be strong."

Oliver made a perfect little home for the caterpillar
in his mummy's bedroom.

Every morning he carefully drew back the curtains
and let the bright sunshine pour in. And every
morning the caterpillar crawled over to greet Oliver
when he brought fresh fruit for him and his mummy.

"Mummy!" said Oliver. "The caterpillar is getting bigger!"

"That's because you've helped him to get stronger,"
said his mummy.

The caterpillar ate and ate
and ate.
And he grew and grew
and grew.

"You're getting so big!"
Oliver smiled. "We'll have
to make you a bigger
home soon."

Oliver studied the pot and noticed the caterpillar had started to weave a silk-like thread around itself. He hoped his mummy was strong enough to come to the window to see.

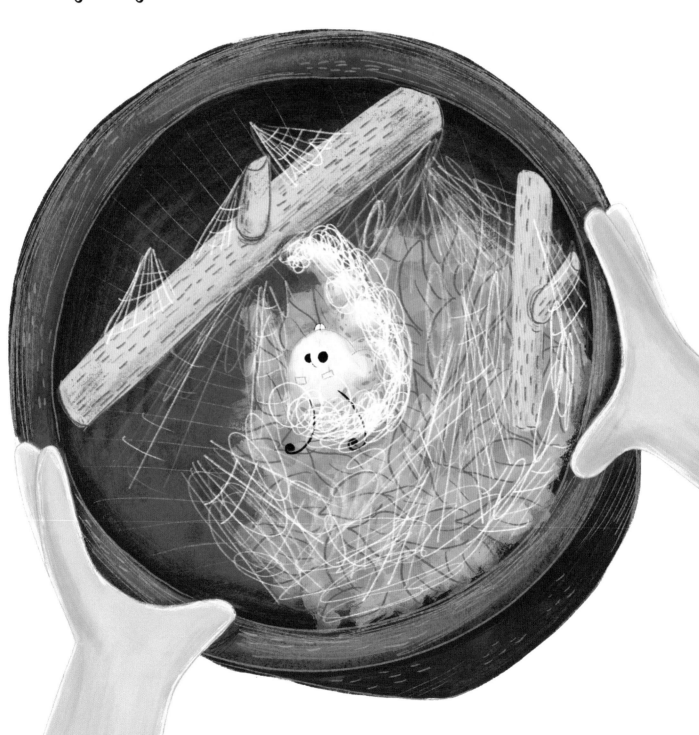

The next morning Oliver pulled back the curtains as usual.
But this morning was different. His mummy was sitting up.
"Oliver, would you like me to help you feed
your caterpillar today?" she asked.
"Are you feeling stronger?" smiled Oliver.
"I'm starting to," replied his mummy.
"Just like your caterpillar.
Thank you for looking after me too."

Oliver took the plate of juicy fruit over to the caterpillar.

He couldn't wait to see his friend crawl out to greet him.

But the caterpillar wasn't there. Tears streamed down Oliver's face.

"He's gone!" he cried. "He didn't say goodbye."

"Oliver," said his mummy, "look inside the lid."
Something was hanging down in a brown crispy looking skin.
"It's a chrysalis," said his mummy. "The caterpillar is getting ready to
turn into a butterfly! Soon it will be time for him to fly."
"Just like when you used to lift me up to fly!" asked Oliver.
"Yes," sighed his mummy. "I hope I can do that again soon."

Oliver kept checking if the butterfly had emerged from its chrysalis. Oliver longed to see his friend again! But the days and nights went by so slowly.

"I hope the fruit has made you strong enough to come out soon," he whispered.

"It's helping *me*," said Oliver's mummy as she slowly walked towards him. He smiled and hugged her tightly.

The next morning, Oliver drew back the curtains, and there was the butterfly!

Its wings flapped slowly. Orange, brown, black and white colours shone in the bright sun light.

"Oliver," said his mummy, "soon your butterfly will need to spread his wings and fly outside."

"Oh, I wish he could stay here, Mummy," said Oliver.

"But he is stronger now," she said. "He needs to be free."

Oliver thought about the other butterflies he had seen flying outside and how happy and free they looked. He thought about his mummy out of bed, free from her tiredness.

Oliver picked up the pot and carried it carefully to the flowers in the garden. He opened it and let the butterfly walk on to his hand.

"I'll never forget you," he whispered to his friend.

"I hope you don't forget me."

Oliver lifted up the butterfly and he flew high out of his hands, swooping and swerving through the air. His wings flapped furiously like excited arms waving goodbye.

Weeks went by. Oliver looked for his friend every day. Until one afternoon in the garden, something caught his eye. A flash of orange, brown, black and white, shone in the sunlight. It swooped and swerved and landed on his arm.

Oliver called to his mummy excitedly. "The butterfly came back!"

"Do you know why?" said his mummy. "Because you kept hope."

"What is hope?" asked Oliver.

"Hope is the power to think anything is possible," she replied.

She scooped Oliver up into her arms . . .
"You can lift me again, Mummy!" exclaimed Oliver.

"Yes," she smiled, raising him high in the air,
swooshing and swooping him.
Oliver felt so happy to be flying in his mummy's arms again.
He never wanted it to stop.
At that moment, his butterfly took flight . . .

but Oliver just smiled as his friend flew away.
He knew he would be back again and that
his mummy would find the strength for
them to keep flying together.
Because Oliver had hope.

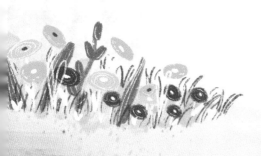

The End